Australia

by Rachel Anne Cantor

Consultant: Marjorie Faulstich Orellana, PhD
Professor of Urban Schooling
University of California, Los Angeles

BEARPORT
PUBLISHING

New York, New York

Credits

Cover, © robert cicchetti/Shutterstock and © Yobro10/iStock; TOC, © Ashwin/Shutterstock; 4, © swissmediavision/iStock; 5T, © wavebreakmedia/Shutterstock; 5B, © CraigRJD/iStock; 7, © CandyAppleRed Images/Alamy Stock Photo; 8, © Bossiema/iStock; 9T, © TonyFeder/iStock; 9B, © Janelle Lugge/Shutterstock; 10–11, © WaterFrame/Alamy Stock Photo; 11R, © buttchi 3 Sha Life/Shutterstock; 12, © John Crux/Shutterstock; 13 (T to B), © Scisetti Alfio/Shutterstock, © Eric Isselee/Shutterstock, and © JohnCarnemolla/iStock; 14, © felixR/iStock; 15, © david franklin/iStock; 16T, © Werner Forman Archive/Bridgeman Images; 16B, © Rafael Ben-Ari/Alamy Stock Photo; 17, © Marine Deswarte/Shutterstock; 18, © Private Collection/Bridgeman Images; 19, © XiXinXing/iStock; 20, © tap10/iStock; 21, © bikeriderlondon/Shutterstock; 22–23, © Paolo Bona/Shutterstock; 23R, © Beata Jancsik/Shutterstock; 24, © robertharding/Alamy Stock Photo; 25T, © mirjana ristic damjanovic/Shutterstock; 25B, © robynmac/iStock; 26, © galit seligmann/Alamy Stock Photo; 27T, © Kokkai Ng/iStock; 27B, © fotohunter/Shutterstock; 28–29, © tsvibrav/iStock; 30T, © Wojciechkozlowski/Dreamstime, © Robyn Mackenzie/Dreamstime, and © Asafta/Dreamstime; 30B, © CraigRJD/iStock; 31 (T to B), © Daniiielc/iStock, © Intrepix/Shutterstock, © SARAWUT KUNDEJ/Shutterstock, © XiXinXing/iStock, and © Marine Deswarte/Shutterstock; 32, © tristan tan/Shutterstock.

Publisher: Kenn Goin
Editor: Jessica Rudolph
Creative Director: Spencer Brinker
Design: Debrah Kaiser
Photo Researcher: Thomas Persano

Library of Congress Cataloging-in-Publication Data

Names: Cantor, Rachel Anne, author.
Title: Australia / by Rachel Anne Cantor.
Description: New York, New York : Bearport Publishing, [2018] | Series: Countries we come from | Includes bibliographical references and index. | Audience: Ages 5–8.
Identifiers: LCCN 2017012310 (print) | LCCN 2017013041 (ebook) | ISBN 9781684023066 (ebook) | ISBN 9781684022526 (library binding)
Subjects: LCSH: Australia—Juvenile literature.
Classification: LCC DU96 (ebook) | LCC DU96 .C35 2018 (print) | DDC 994—dc23
LC record available at https://lccn.loc.gov/2017012310

For more information, write to Bearport Publishing Company, Inc., 45 West 21st Street, Suite 3B, New York, New York 10010. Printed in the United States of America.

10 9 8 7 6 5 4 3 2 1

Contents

Adventurous

4

Friendly

WILD

Australia is a huge country located between the Indian and Pacific oceans.

It's also one of the seven **continents** on Earth.

About 23 million people live there.

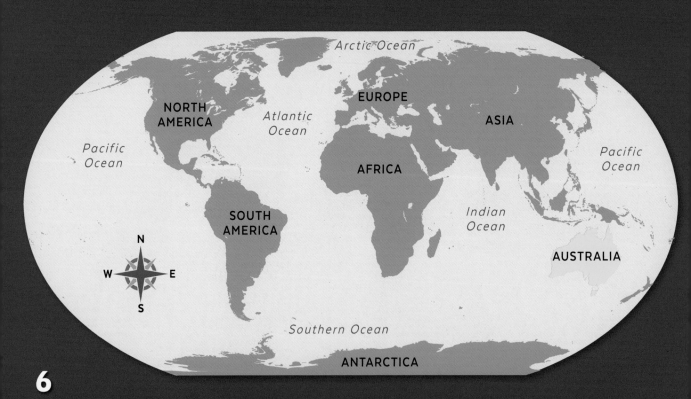

Australian people are also known as "Aussies."

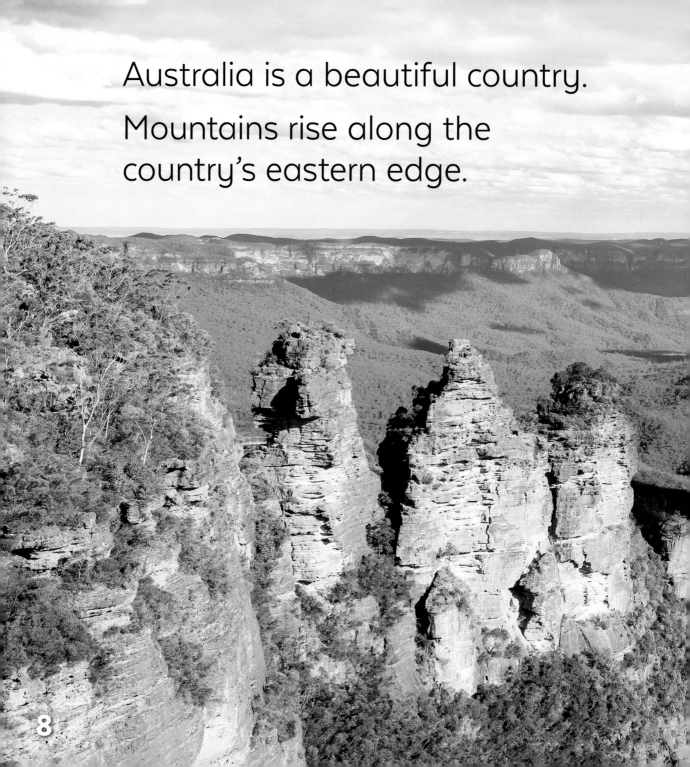

Australia is a beautiful country.

Mountains rise along the country's eastern edge.

In the center of Australia is a giant desert called the Outback.

Sandy beaches surround Australia's coasts.

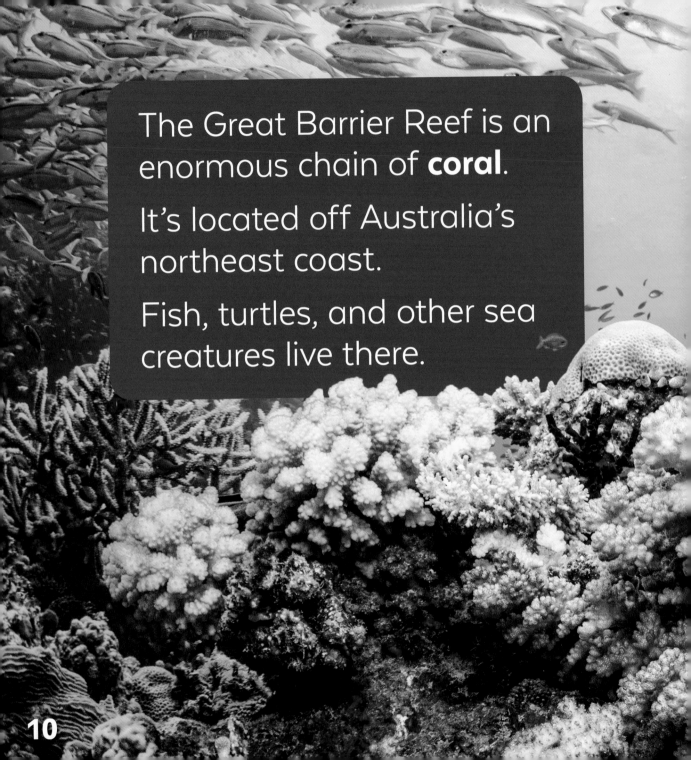

The Great Barrier Reef is an enormous chain of **coral**.

It's located off Australia's northeast coast.

Fish, turtles, and other sea creatures live there.

Rising temperatures have damaged parts of the reef. Scientists are trying to keep the rest of it safe.

damaged coral

Many animals in Australia are found nowhere else on Earth.

Kangaroos live throughout the country.

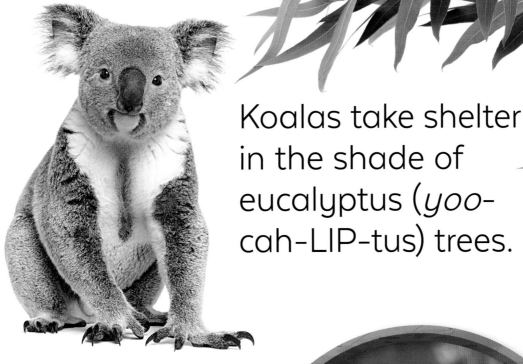

Koalas take shelter in the shade of eucalyptus (*yoo-cah-LIP-tus*) trees.

The platypus has webbed feet and a duck-like bill. Most mammals give birth to live young, but platypuses lay eggs!

13

The **capital** of Australia is Canberra.

The country's largest city is Sydney. About five million people live there!

The Sydney Opera House is a famous building. Its white concrete domes, or shells, face Sydney Harbor.

Aboriginal and Torres Strait Islander people have lived in Australia for more than 50,000 years!

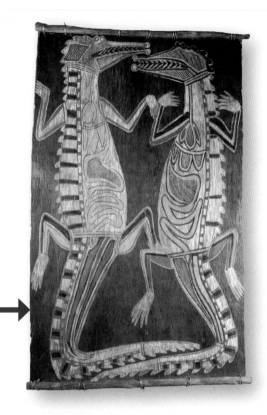

bark painting

painted boomerang

Their carvings, paintings, and other artworks are known throughout the world.

Uluru is a spectacular rock formation in central Australia. It's a **sacred** place for the Anangu Aboriginal people.

In the late 1700s, English people began settling in Australia.

By the 1820s, other Europeans had begun moving there.

Unfortunately, some Europeans hurt and killed many Aboriginal people.

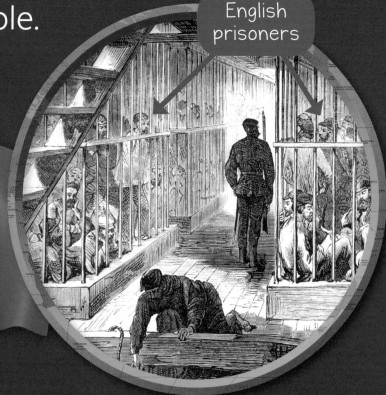

English prisoners

From 1788 to 1868, England sent more than 160,000 prisoners to Australia!

Today, **immigrants** from China, India, the United States, and many other countries live in Australia.

Most Aussies speak English.

However, Australians and Americans have different ways of saying certain things.

Here's how to say hello to a friend:

G'day, mate!
(guh-DAY MAYT)

After English, the most common languages in Australia are Mandarin, Italian, and Arabic.

Many Aussies love to play rugby!

The sport is similar to American football, but most players don't wear helmets or padding.

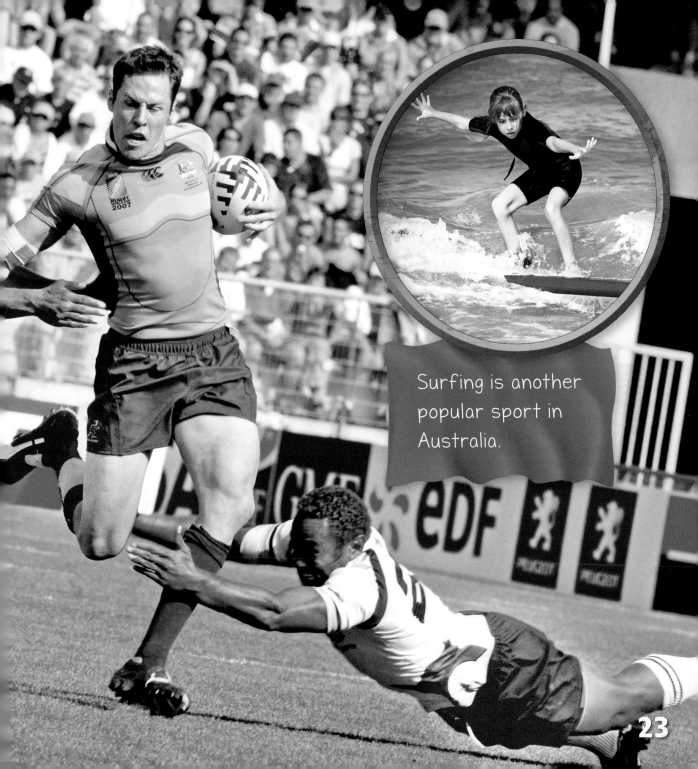

Surfing is another popular sport in Australia.

23

Many Australians enjoy getting together for barbecue meals.

Aussie barbecues are nicknamed "barbies!"

They can include grilled beef, chicken, shrimp, or sausage.

For dessert, try a Lamington! It's a yummy sponge cake covered in chocolate and coconut.

In December, many Australians celebrate Christmas.

Most of the country is warm during this time of year.

People often celebrate on the beach!

In Australia, the day after Christmas is Boxing Day. People give gifts to workers, such as mail carriers.

Each year, more than five million people visit Australia.

Many visitors drive along the Great Ocean Road for its gorgeous views.

The Great Ocean Road stretches for 151 miles (243 km) along the southeastern coast.

Fast Facts

Capital city: Canberra

Population of Australia: About 23 million

Main language: English

Money: Australian dollar

Major religion: Christianity

Nearby countries: Papua New Guinea, Indonesia, New Zealand

Cool Fact: Australia is home to a large flightless bird called the cassowary. It has powerful legs that can deliver dangerous kicks to enemies.

capital (KAP-uh-tuhl) a city where a country's government is based

continents (KON-tuh-nuhnts) the world's seven large land masses—Africa, Antarctica, Asia, Australia, Europe, North America, and South America

coral (KORE-uhl) an ocean habitat formed from the skeletons of tiny sea animals called coral polyps

immigrants (IM-uh-gruhnts) people who move from one country to live in a new one

sacred (SAY-krid) holy, religious

31

Index

Read More

Friedman, Mel. *Australia and Oceania (A True Book).* New York: Scholastic (2009).

Sexton, Colleen. *Australia (Blastoff! Readers: Exploring Countries).* Minneapolis, MN: Bellwether Media (2016).

Learn More Online

To learn more about Australia, visit
www.bearportpublishing.com/CountriesWeComeFrom

About the Author

Rachel Anne Cantor is a writer who lives
in Boston, Massachusetts. She hopes
to visit Australia very soon.

DATE DUE

FOLLETT